JOURNEY

Aaron Becker

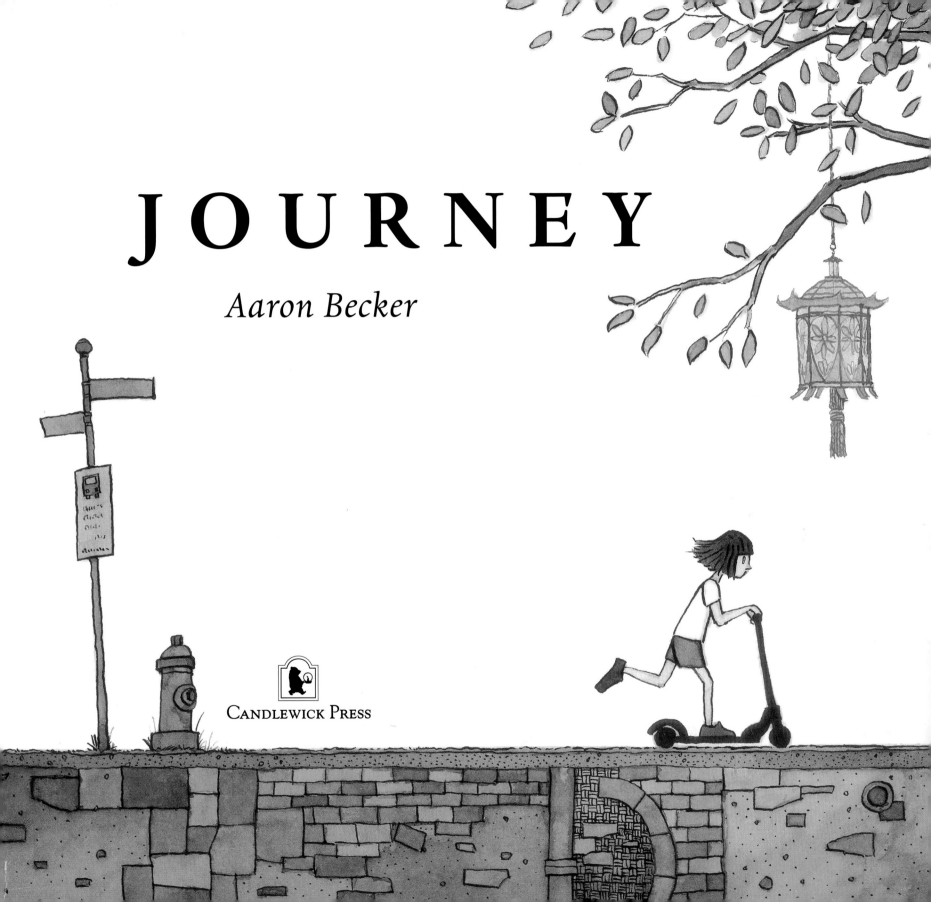

CANDLEWICK PRESS

For Josephine

This book would not have been possible without the help of some great
friends and colleagues, notably Joanne Taylor, Laurel Snyder, David Costello,
Diane deGroat, Jeff Mack, Linda Pratt, Maryellen Hanley, Mary Lee Donovan,
and last but not least, my wife, Darci Palmquist.

Copyright © 2013 by Aaron Becker

First edition 2013

Library of Congress Catalog Card Number 2012947264
ISBN 978-0-7636-6053-6

TLF 18
20

Printed in Dongguan, Guangdong, China

The illustrations were done in watercolor and pen and ink.

Candlewick Press
99 Dover Street
Somerville, Massachusetts 02144

visit us at www.candlewick.com

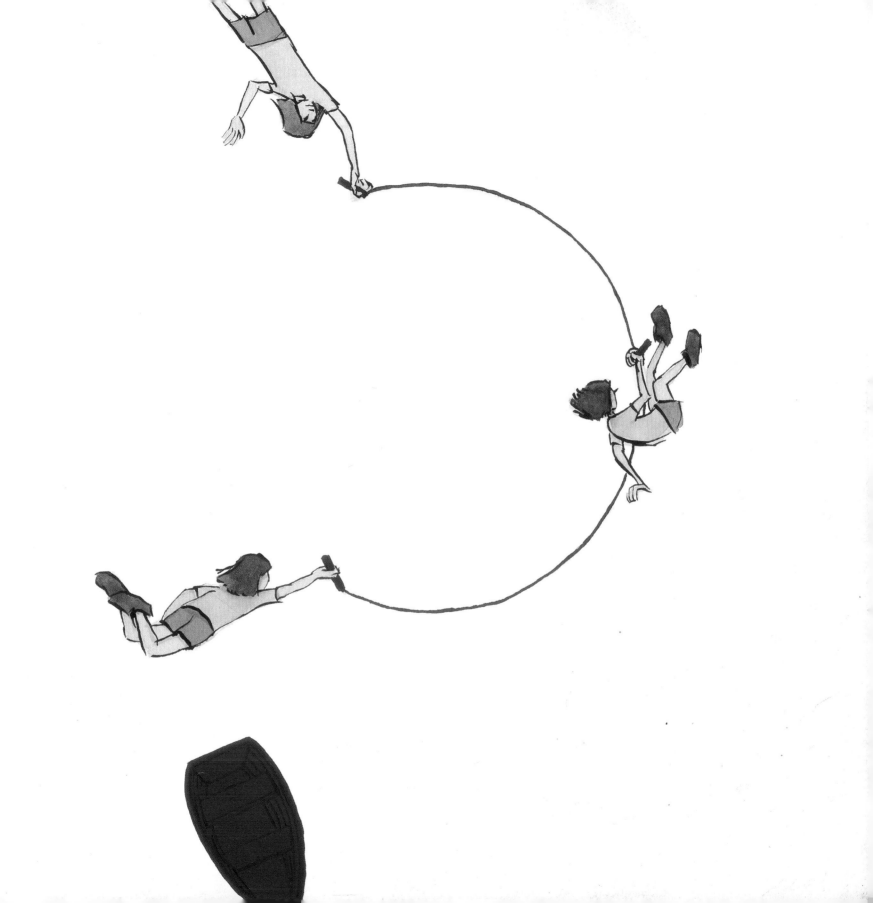